Maddie
the Fun and Games
Fairy

Special thanks to
Rachel Elliot

No part of this publication may be reproduced, stored in a retrieval system, or transmitted in any form or by any means, electronic, mechanical, photocopying, recording, or otherwise, without written permission of the publisher. For information regarding permission, write to Rainbow Magic Limited c/o HIT Entertainment, 830 South Greenville Avenue, Allen, TX 75002-3320.

ISBN 978-0-545-43395-2

12 11 10 9 8 7 6 5 4 3 2 1   12 13 14 15 16 17/0

Printed in China   68

First Scholastic printing, August 2012

Maddie
the Fun and Games Fairy

by Daisy Meadows

SCHOLASTIC INC.

New York   Toronto   London   Auckland
Sydney   Mexico City   New Delhi   Hong Kong

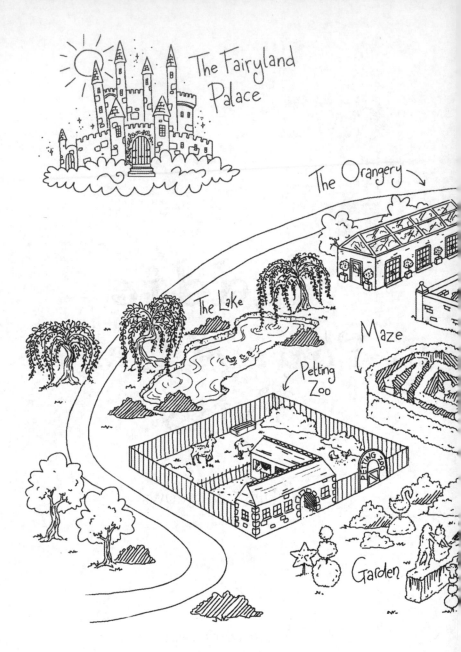

The Fairyland Palace

The Orangery

The Lake

Maze

Petting Zoo

PETTING ZOO

Garden

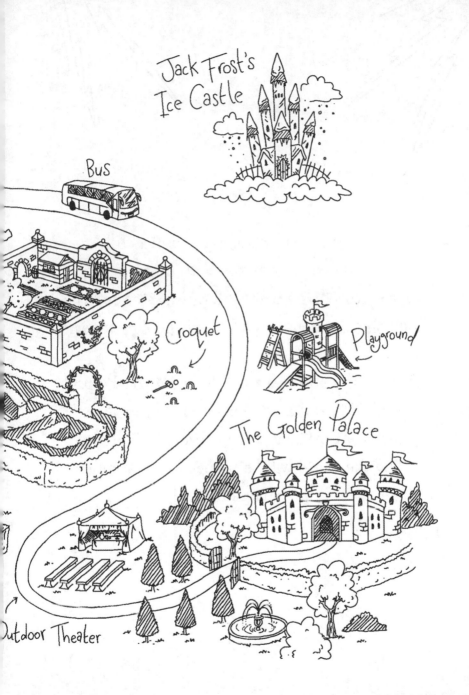

The fairies are planning a magical ball,
With guests of honor and fun for all.
They're expecting a night full of laughter and cheer,
But they'll get a shock when my goblins appear!

Adventures and treats will be things of the past,
And I'll beat those troublesome fairies at last.
My iciest magic will blast through the room
And the world will be plunged into grimness
and gloom!

Contents

Temper Tantrums

"I've never seen such beautiful toys!" gasped Rachel Walker, gazing around with wide eyes.

"I can imagine the princes and princesses playing with them when they lived here long ago," agreed her best friend, Kirsty Tate.

The girls were standing in the royal playroom at the top of one of the Golden Palace's towers, where they were staying for a Royal Sleepover Camp. The other kids were already kneeling down beside the toys, choosing what they wanted to play with. There was a model steam engine that ran along a track around the room, a large jar full of swirly glass marbles, and boxes filled with puzzles and wooden spinning tops. Pretty china

dolls sat on low shelves beside plump teddy bears, and balls of every size and color rolled around their feet.

"Oh, Rachel, look!" cried Kirsty. On a low table in one corner of the room stood an exact miniature copy of the Golden Palace. It had the same gleaming white stone walls and golden turrets. Tiny flags fluttered from the top of each tower. Rachel and Kirsty carefully opened the front wall to look inside. The rooms were exactly the same as those in the real palace, with thick carpets and plush furniture. There were dolls dressed in royal robes, plus maids and butlers, too.

"This must be the princess," said Rachel, picking up a tiny girl doll with flowing golden hair and a sparkling tiara.

"She reminds me of Lizzie the Sweet Treats Fairy," whispered Kirsty.

The girls smiled at each other, thinking about their wonderful secret. They were good friends with the fairies, and often had magical adventures in Fairyland! Since they had arrived at the Golden Palace, they had been helping the Princess Fairies find their tiaras, which Jack Frost and his goblins had stolen.

Suddenly, there was a shout from one of the other kids. When Rachel and Kirsty turned around, they saw Katie and Maya each holding on to one arm of a china doll.

"This one's mine!" Katie shouted.

"Let go!" Maya shouted back. "I was playing with her first!"

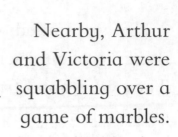

Nearby, Arthur and Victoria were squabbling over a game of marbles. An argument had broken out between the kids playing with a puzzle, and one boy was almost in tears because the older kids wouldn't let him play with the train.

Kirsty and Rachel exchanged a worried glance.

"It's all because Princess Maddie lost her magical tiara," Kirsty whispered.

The Princess Fairies needed their tiaras to make sure that everyone in the human and fairy worlds had a happy and magical time. Maddie was the Fun and Games Fairy. Without her tiara, no one could share well or even be a good teammate when they played games.

Jack Frost had taken the tiaras into the human world, but Queen Titania had cast a spell so that they would end up in the Golden Palace, where Kirsty and Rachel could help find them. So far, they had tracked down five of the tiaras.

"We need to find Maddie's tiara quickly," said Kirsty, looking around the playroom at the grumpy, arguing kids.

"All we can do is keep our eyes open for clues," said Rachel. "We have to wait for the magic to find us! Come on, let's try one of these old-fashioned games."

Kirsty picked up a strangely shaped wooden toy. It looked like a cup with a ball attached to it by a string. The girls soon realized that they had to try to catch the ball in the cup.

"Let's take turns," said Rachel. "I'll go first."

Suddenly, Kirsty felt her forehead crease into a frown.

"Why should you go first?" she asked. "*I* chose the game."

Rachel didn't reply, but she frowned as well. She swung the ball and tried to catch it in the cup, but missed completely.

"That was your fault," she snapped. "You distracted me!"

"I should have gone first," said Kirsty

with a pout. "It's not fair!"

Suddenly, Rachel dropped the toy and
the girls stared at each other, horrified.

"We never argue!" said Kirsty,
her voice trembling a little. "What's
wrong?"

"It must be because of the missing
tiara," said Rachel. "Even *we* can't play
well together!"

"I'm sorry," said Kirsty. "I didn't mean
to argue with you."

"I didn't, either," said Rachel. "I'm
sorry, too."

Just then, Kirsty noticed something out
of the corner of her eye.

"Rachel, look—there's a light inside
the little palace!" she exclaimed. "What
could it be?"

A Miniature Surprise

The girls knelt down beside the model
of the palace. Sure enough, a twinkling
light was moving around inside. They
put their eyes up to the tiny windows,
trying to follow the light.

"It's in the library!" murmured Rachel
in a low voice. "No, wait, it's moving up
the stairs."

"I can see it!" whispered Kirsty. "It's going through the portrait gallery . . . and up the stairs again!"

Rachel peeked into the model through a different window.

"It's in the playroom!" she said. "It's so bright that I can hardly look at it!"

The light stopped beside a tiny model rocking horse. Then it faded slightly, and the girls saw Maddie the Fun and Games Fairy sitting on the rocking horse and waving at them!

"Hello, girls!" she said in her cheery voice. "I've come to help you look for my tiara—oh!"

She cried out as the rocking horse gave a sudden lurch. She tumbled off and landed on the floor with a bump.

"Ouch!" she said, picking herself up and smoothing out her shorts and vest. "That's what happens without my magical tiara—playtime stops being fun."

"We know," whispered Rachel. "Playing with all these toys is supposed to be a treat, but everyone is just arguing."

Just then the playroom door opened and two palace directors, Louis and Caroline, walked in, smiling. But the smiles left their faces as they looked around the room.

"What's wrong?" asked Louis. "Why is everyone arguing?"

The other kids let go of the toys and looked embarrassed. Nobody replied.

"I hope that you'll play better during today's activity," said Caroline. "It's a Golden Palace field day, and the events will be games that princes and princesses used to play many years ago!" The children gave *oohs* and *ahhs* of excitement, but Rachel and Kirsty exchanged a worried look. "Without Maddie's tiara, a day

of playing games could be a disaster," said Kirsty under her breath.

The other kids put away the toys they had played with and left the nursery. Rachel and Kirsty lingered behind until they were alone in the room. Then they quickly opened the front of the little palace and Maddie flew into the hood of Kirsty's sweater. Just in time! Caroline poked her head around the door.

"Come on, girls," she said with a smile. "The others are already getting changed!"

A short while later, everyone was

outside in the palace gardens in their sportswear. Maddie was still hiding in Kirsty's hood. They all gathered around Louis and Caroline, who were standing beside a large gold sports bag with fancy piping around the edges.

"OK, everyone," said Louis. "Please divide into two teams."

The kids formed two groups, laughing excitedly and looking forward to the games. Louis told them that the teams

would be called the Unicorns and the Lions.

"Now we'll pick a captain for each team," said Caroline. "I choose Arthur to be captain of the Lion team."

"And Kirsty will be captain of the Unicorn team," Louis added.

Caroline handed out beautiful satin overshirts for the teams to wear. "These are like the tunics that knights used to wear over their armor," she said. The Unicorns had royal blue and the Lions had red.

Louis picked up his gold sports bag. "I have a wonderful picnic in here for later on," he said. "So let's get started!"

The directors led the way toward the croquet lawn on the far side of the palace gardens.

"Our first event is a croquet match," Caroline said. "The princes and princesses who stayed here would have played this game all the time."

Rachel and Kirsty saw that the grass was dotted with croquet hoops. There were three boys in the middle of the croquet lawn, wearing green warm-up suits and green baseball caps pulled down over their faces.

"Who are you?" asked Arthur. "You can't play here."

The biggest boy clutched his sports

bag to his chest as if it were precious. It looked very much like Louis's gold bag.

"We're not going anywhere," he said in a gruff voice.

The other kids looked very frustrated.

"Go away," said Katie.

"You're not welcome here," said Victoria.

"I'm surprised at all of you," said Caroline. "Part of playing together is not letting anyone feel left out."

The kids looked kind of ashamed, but they didn't apologize. Rachel and

Kirsty guessed that the missing tiara was turning them into bad sports.

"Are you visiting the Golden Palace for the day?" Caroline asked the boys.

The boys glanced at one another. One of them nodded.

"Then we'd like to invite you to join

our field day as a third team," said
Caroline.

The boys didn't look very excited, but
Caroline handed out the croquet mallets
and balls. Louis blew his whistle, and
the game began!

Goblin Games

They hadn't been playing for very long when Arthur gave an angry yell.

"Cheater!" he shouted.

"Oh, no," said Rachel.

"It's starting," said Maddie. "The game's going all wrong."

The new boys were hitting the hoops with their mallets and kicking the ball with their big feet.

"Stop it!" Victoria shouted.

"Why are those boys being so terrible?" asked Rachel with a frown. "It's almost as if—"

She paused as one of the boys laughed  and tossed his baseball hat into the air. For a moment, they saw his face. It was green! "Goblins!" Kirsty exclaimed in alarm. The goblins were scampering around the croquet lawn with glee, the other kids were shouting and complaining, and Louis and Caroline were trying to calm everyone down. It was chaos!

"We won!" the biggest goblin chanted as he danced around in a circle. "We won!"

He put down his
sports bag and did
cartwheels all
around the
big lawn.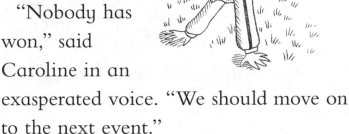

"Nobody has
won," said
Caroline in an
exasperated voice. "We should move on
to the next event."

The biggest goblin stopped doing
cartwheels and staggered dizzily toward
his gold sports bag.

"Not fair!" he grumbled.

Louis picked up his gold bag. "I think
we should do a hoop-and-stick race
around the lake now," he said. "It should
be lots of fun, so there better not be any
more arguing!"

As Louis and Caroline led the way to the lake, they explained that a long time ago, kids used to play with hoops and sticks all the time.

"You have to keep the hoop rolling along the ground by using the stick," said Caroline. "The path goes all the way around the lake. The first team to get all its players around the lake is the winner."

There weren't enough hoops and sticks for all the kids, so Rachel and Kirsty offered to sit the event out. Louis and Caroline agreed, and Rachel winked at Kirsty.

"This might give us a chance to find Maddie's tiara," she whispered.

"I hope so!" Kirsty replied.

Louis put his bag down and showed

the kids how to keep the hoop moving along by tapping it gently with the stick. Because they weren't taking a turn, the girls stepped aside.

As they looked around, they noticed that two of the goblins seemed to be having an argument. The biggest goblin was standing almost nose-to-nose with a short freckled goblin, frowning and bickering. The freckled goblin pointed to the bag in the arms of the biggest goblin. Then he jabbed his long green finger toward the bag that Louis had just put down.

"The goblins

seem really worried about the bags,"
said Kirsty thoughtfully. "I wonder if
they mixed up their bag with Louis's
bag. They look almost exactly the
same."

"But why would they be so angry
about that?" Rachel wondered aloud.
"Unless there was something inside that
they didn't want Louis to see . . ."

"Like my tiara!" exclaimed Maddie.

The girls stared at each other in alarm.

Of course! The
goblins must have
hidden the tiara
in their sports
bag, and the
biggest goblin
accidentally picked up Louis's bag
instead!

Just then, Louis blew his whistle and
the race began. One of the goblins was
running along eagerly among the kids,
spinning his hoop along with his stick.
But the biggest goblin and the freckled
goblin started to sneak toward Louis's
bag.

"Quick!" exclaimed Rachel urgently.
"We have to reach that bag before the
goblins do!"

"And before Louis and Caroline unzip the bag and find the tiara inside," Kirsty added. "They'd probably take it to the palace's lost and found, or the police, and we'd never be able to get it back."

"What are we going to do?" asked Maddie, her big eyes brimming with tears of concern.

The girls cast anxious glances at the goblins, who were getting closer and closer to the bag.

"I have an idea," said Kirsty. "Let's ask Caroline if we can set up for the picnic, so she'll give us the bag. We can get the tiara back and then tell her that the bags got switched."

As the hoop race wound around the lake, Rachel and Kirsty hurried up to the palace director.

"Caroline, could we help set up the picnic?" Rachel asked.

"Of course," said Caroline, her eyes fixed on the race. "Just as soon as our field day is over."

The girls looked at each other in panic. By then it would be too late!

A Daring Plan

The two goblins were now standing next to Louis's bag. The biggest goblin stretched out his hand, ready to swap the bags.

"I can't watch," said Rachel, closing her eyes.

But at that moment, Caroline looked around and noticed the goblins.

"Hold it!" she said. "You're not

allowed to start the picnic until the field day events are over. Be patient, boys!"

Rachel, Kirsty, and Maddie let out long sighs of relief. That was close! "We have to think of a way to reach that bag without the goblins or Caroline stopping us," said Kirsty.

"I have a plan," said Rachel eagerly. "Caroline is busy watching the race. Maddie, could you turn us into fairies? We could distract the goblins while you fly to the bag and take the tiara."

"That's a great plan!" said Maddie.

They darted behind a bush and Maddie waved her wand. There was a puff of glittering fairy dust, and the girls felt themselves shrinking to fairy-size. Delicate wings appeared on their backs, and they fluttered them in delight.

"I'll distract the third goblin," said Kirsty.

She zoomed after the goblin who was

participating in the hoop race. He was
rolling his hoop near the edge of the
lake, so Kirsty flew close to the water,
weaving her way through the reeds and
the trailing branches of the weeping
willows that lined the lake. Luckily, the
other kids were not close by, so it was
easy to keep out of sight.

As the goblin's hoop rolled close to the reeds, Kirsty darted out and flicked it away, making sure that the goblin saw her. He yelled with rage.

"You pesky fairy! Leave my hoop alone!"

Kirsty tapped the hoop again, sending it rolling toward the maze where the girls had had their adventure with Princess Hope the Happiness Fairy. Kirsty flew next to the hoop, keeping it rolling swiftly along.

"You come back here *now*!" demanded

the goblin, chasing after her. "That's right, follow me as fast as you can," said Kirsty under her breath. "It's all up to Rachel and Maddie now!"

Rachel had been thinking hard about how to distract the other two goblins.

"When Kirsty and I were in the royal playroom, we were playing with a cup-and-ball game," she told Maddie. "Maybe if you could use your magic to make something like that, it would take the goblins' minds off the bags."

She described the game to Maddie, who nodded and waved her wand. At

once, two sets of the cup-and-ball game
appeared on the grass between the
goblins and the bag.

Caroline was still watching the race,
with her back to them.

"I'll keep the goblins distracted while
you get your tiara," said Rachel.
"Good luck!"

"Good luck to you, too," said Maddie,
giving her a hug. "I think you and
Kirsty are really brave."

Rachel smiled
and slipped
quickly inside
one of the cups.

"What's that?" she
heard one of the goblins say in surprise.

"It's a toy!" the other goblin exclaimed,
picking it up.

Rachel darted out of the cup and the goblin gave a squawk of surprise. "It's one of those tricky fairies!" he squealed. "Catch her!"

Rachel flitted and zoomed around and around the goblins, keeping just out of reach of their grabby hands. They looked like giant frogs as they leaped into the air and stretched out their scrawny arms, trying to reach her.

The goblins did a lot of shouting and yelping, but luckily Caroline was just out of earshot.

As Rachel was drawing the goblins
farther and farther away from the bag,
Maddie was getting closer to it. She
stayed close to the ground, hiding herself
among the thick blades of grass. The
bag was near Caroline's feet, and

Caroline was hopping around in excitement, cheering for the teams. A few times, Maddie had to flit sideways to avoid Caroline's feet, and that made it difficult to reach the bag.

At that moment, shouts and applause broke out. The race had finished! The goblins spun around, forgetting all about Rachel.

"Now's our chance!" one of the goblins said to the other.

As Caroline hurried to congratulate

the winners, the goblin sprinted toward the bag. Rachel zoomed in front of him and darted back and forth, trying to distract him, but he just batted her away with his hand. Rachel could only watch in horror as he swapped the bags without Caroline noticing a thing. The goblins had the tiara back!

What could Kirsty and Rachel do now?

Bag Swap

Kirsty returned from the maze just in time to see the Lions win the hoop race. She glimpsed Maddie and Rachel hiding behind the bush, and flew over to join them. Their sad faces told her that they hadn't been able to get the tiara.

"The goblins have the bag," Rachel said. "How are we going to get the tiara back now?"

The Unicorn team trudged up to Caroline, looking very disappointed.

"I hate losing," said Katie. "It ruins everything."

"It's taking part in something that counts," Louis said, trying to cheer them up. "You had fun—it doesn't really matter who won."

But the Unicorn team still looked miserable, and the Lions were laughing about having beaten them.

"This is all because my tiara is missing," Maddie told the girls. "No one can enjoy the spirit of the game. The Unicorns feel disappointed that they lost, and the Lions are just gloating."

At that moment, Caroline clapped her hands together and asked for quiet.

"For the final sports activity of the day, we are going to have a rowing race across the lake," she said. "It's very shallow, so we have some special small rowboats for you to use."

She pointed to where several brightly

painted rowboats bobbed in the shining water.

"Could the team captains come forward now to lead their boats?" Caroline asked.

"Oh!" Kirsty gasped. "I'm the captain of the Unicorns. I have to go!"

Maddie quickly changed Kirsty back to human-size, and she hurried out from

behind the bush to join Arthur and the
biggest goblin. The teams climbed on
board and Kirsty took her place at
the front of the Unicorns' boat, which
was sky blue. The Lions' boat was
sunshine yellow.

"Come on," said Maddie. "Let's go
down to the lake and watch the race."

She and Rachel flew down and hid
among the reeds, watching as the
goblins climbed into the green boat.
The third goblin had found his way
back from the maze just in time! Rachel
could hear that they were still arguing,
even though they had the tiara back.

"It's all your fault that we've lost both
events so far," grumbled the freckled
goblin to the biggest goblin. "Thanks to
you, we almost lost the tiara. Jack Frost

would have punished all of us."

"Oh, shut your mouth," said the biggest goblin rudely. "I want to win this rowing race—those silly humans must not beat us."

"Just hold on to the bag this time," said the third goblin.

The biggest goblin opened his mouth to argue, but just then the freckled goblin shoved an oar into his hands and Louis blew his whistle.

The final race had begun!

The three boats pulled out toward the opposite bank of the lake. Rachel and Maddie could see Kirsty in the front of the sky-blue boat, eagerly cheering for her team.

In the front of the sunshine-yellow boat, Arthur was urging his team on. His boat was neck and neck with Kirsty's.

"Come on, Unicorns!" said Rachel, wishing that she were with them. "You can do it!"

The green boat was just behind the others, and Maddie and Rachel saw that an argument had started among the goblins. Their voices echoed clearly across the water.

"This is *my* oar!" yelled the freckled goblin. "Let go!"

"You're pulling in the wrong direction!" shouted the third goblin.

"How would you know?" demanded the biggest goblin, paddling furiously with his oar.

The boat began to go around in circles, spinning faster and faster. The goblins yelled louder and louder, shoving one another and fighting over the oars.

The boat rocked dangerously from side
to side.

"Boys, stop fooling around!" Louis
called from the side of the lake.

But they ignored him, and the freckled
goblin stood up to try to yank the oar
out of the third
goblin's hands.
He gave one
huge tug . . .
and the boat
turned over
in the water!
There was
a huge splash
as the goblins
and the bag
plunged into
the lake.
"Now's our chance!" said Maddie.
She gave a little flick of her wand,
and a breathing bubble immediately
appeared, covering Rachel's head

completely and then disappearing with
a gentle *pop*! Rachel knew from her
adventures with Shannon the Ocean
Fairy that this meant she would be able
to breathe underwater.

"Let's go!" Rachel said.

Side by side, Rachel
and Maddie dove
into the sparkling
lake water and
zoomed toward
the place where
the goblins had
fallen in. They could see three pairs of
lanky green legs standing on the lake
bottom—and next to them was the gold
sports bag!

Bickering, Boats, and Bubbles

The goblins were still shaking lake water out of their eyes and ears when Rachel and Maddie reached the bag and pulled open the zipper. Rachel looked up and saw a big green hand reaching down toward the bag.

She pointed urgently, and Maddie swam into the bag at lightning speed.

Half a second later, Maddie zoomed out with the tiara, which had shrunk to fairy-size as soon as she had touched it.

As the goblin's hand found the bag, Rachel and Maddie darted back toward the reeds. They flew out of the water, and Rachel turned to Maddie, her eyes shining.

"We did it!" she said happily. "You got your tiara back!"

Maddie rested her tiara on top of her long dark braids and smiled at Rachel. "I was afraid I had lost it forever!" she said.

She turned to look at the goblins,

who were sloshing their way out of the shallow water. As Maddie and Rachel watched, the freckled one peeked into the bag and then glared at the biggest goblin. Then he put his whole head into the bag, and finally turned it upside down and shook it.

The biggest goblin grabbed the bag and jumped up and down on top of it a few times. Then he stomped away from the lake, followed by the other two goblins. They disappeared among a

group of trees, and Rachel heaved a sigh
of relief.

"Thank goodness they're gone!"
she said.

The two fairies flew under the
dangling branches of a weeping willow,
and Maddie turned Rachel back
to human-size. Then she hid inside
Rachel's shorts pocket, and Rachel ran
to watch the end of the boat race.

Everyone suddenly seemed much more cheerful. Rachel could hear them all cheering their teammates on.

"Now that my tiara is back where it belongs, everyone is being a good sport again," said Maddie with a happy laugh.

"Come on, Unicorns!" called Rachel in her loudest voice. "You can do it!"

The boats were still neck and neck, but when Rachel shouted, the sky-blue boat seemed to gain an extra burst of speed. Its bow pushed onto the gravel on the bank just ahead of the sunshine-yellow boat.

"We won!" Kirsty cheered.

"Nice race, Unicorns!" said Arthur.

Louis and Caroline came toward them, clapping their hands and smiling.

"What an exciting finish!" said Louis. "The Unicorn team just won, so that makes one victory for each team."

"Field day is a tie!" added Caroline.

The two teams helped each other out of their boats, sharing congratulations and patting one another on the back. Kirsty ran up to Rachel and gave her a big hug.

"Kirsty, we got the tiara back,"

Rachel whispered in excitement.

"I already guessed that!" said Kirsty with a laugh. "Halfway through the race, the whole mood changed. Everyone started to be good sports—at last!"

While the teams were making their way to the patch of grass where Louis had set out the picnic, Rachel told Kirsty what had happened. Under the cover of the weeping willow, Maddie fluttered out of Rachel's pocket, wearing a big smile—and her tiara!

"Thank you both for everything you did for me today," she said. "I need to go back to Fairyland now and tell the other Princess Fairies what happened."

"Good-bye, Maddie," said Rachel, smiling at the fairy.

"We really enjoyed helping you find your tiara," Kirsty added warmly. Maddie waved at them both, and then disappeared in a twinkle of silvery sparkles.

Rachel and Kirsty ran to join the other kids, who were just sitting down on a large picnic blanket. Louis and Caroline presented each of them with a gold medal for taking part. On one side was an engraved picture of the Golden Palace, and on the other side were the words:

Golden Palace Field Day Champion

"There's only one thing left for you to do," Louis announced. "Eat!"

As they munched on the delicious picnic, Kirsty smiled at her best friend.

"There's only one more day left at the Golden Palace," she said.

"And one more tiara to find," Rachel added. "It must belong to Eva the Enchanted Ball Fairy. I wonder what adventures we'll have with her!"

Rachel and Kirsty have helped
all of the other Princess Fairies find their tiaras.
Now it's time for them to help

Eva
the Enchanted Ball Fairy!

Join their final princess fairy adventure
in this special sneak peek. . . .

A Dancing Disaster

"One-two-three, one-two-three, one-two-three," murmured Rachel Walker under her breath, trying to concentrate on what her feet were doing. She and her best friend, Kirsty Tate, were staying at the Golden Palace for a Royal Sleepover Camp. Today, they were in the ballroom, enjoying a dance lesson.

The ballroom was beautiful, with huge sparkly chandeliers hanging from the ceiling, and dark-red wallpaper that looked like velvet.

It was the last full day of the camp and Kirsty and Rachel had had lots of fun. They'd been on a treasure hunt, taken part in a field day and a pageant, enjoyed a tea party in the palace gardens, and much more. It had been so exciting to stay in a real palace with a drawbridge, moat, and gold-topped towers. Best of all, the girls had also found themselves on more wonderful fairy adventures, this time with the Princess Fairies!

A grand ball was taking place that evening, and everyone was planning on dressing up in their nicest clothes. Louis and Caroline, the directors who had looked after the campers all week, were teaching them the waltz, but nobody was finding it easy.

"Whoops," said one boy, accidentally stepping on his partner's toes.

"Sorry," said a girl as she swung around too quickly and bumped into the person behind her.

"Ow," said Kirsty as she stumbled, knocking against one of the tables at the far end of the room. The table had been decorated with flower arrangements and elegant glass vases filled with colorful candy, ready for the ball that evening. One of the vases fell over, and Kirsty barely caught it before it hit the floor. . . .

RAINBOW magic

These activities are magical!
Play dress-up, send friendship notes, and much more!

◼SCHOLASTIC
www.scholastic.com
www.rainbowmagiconline.com

HIT entertainment

RMACTIV3

RAINBOW magic™

There's Magic in Every Series!

The Rainbow Fairies
The Weather Fairies
The Jewel Fairies
The Pet Fairies
The Fun Day Fairies
The Petal Fairies
The Dance Fairies
The Music Fairies
The Sports Fairies
The Party Fairies
The Ocean Fairies
The Night Fairies
The Magical Animal Fairies
The Princess Fairies

Read them all!

SCHOLASTIC

www.scholastic.com
www.rainbowmagiconline.com

HIT entertainment

RMFAIRY6

SPECIAL EDITION

Three Books in Each One—More Rainbow Magic Fun!

Joy the Summer Vacation Fairy

Holly the Christmas Fairy

Kylie the Carnival Fairy

Stella the Star Fairy

Shannon the Ocean Fairy

Trixie the Halloween Fairy

Gabriella the Snow Kingdom Fairy

Juliet the Valentine Fairy

Mia the Bridesmaid Fairy

Flora the Dress-Up Fairy

Paige the Christmas Play Fairy

Emma the Easter Fairy

Cara the Camp Fairy

Destiny the Rock Star Fairy

Belle the Birthday Fairy

Olympia the Games Fairy

Selena the Sleepover Fairy

Cheryl the Christmas Tree Fairy

◢◣SCHOLASTIC

scholastic.com
rainbowmagiconline.com

HIT entertainment

RMSPECIAL9